Published in 2018 by **Windmill Books**,
an Imprint of Rosen Publishing
29 East 21st Street, New York, NY 10010

Copyright © 2018 Blake Publishing

Cover and text design: Leanne Nobilio
Editor: Vanessa Barker

Photography: All images © Dreamstime
except pp. 5, 18, 19, 21, 24, iStock.

Cataloging-in-Publication Data

Names: Johnson, Rebecca.
Title: Grace the green sea turtle / Rebecca Johnson.
Description: New York : Windmill Books, 2018. | Series:
    Reptile adventures | Includes index.
Identifiers: ISBN 9781508193623 (pbk.) | ISBN 9781508193586
    (library bound) | ISBN 9781508193661 (6 pack)
Subjects: LCSH: Sea turtles--Juvenile literature.
Classification: LCC QL666.C536 J65 2018 | DDC 597.92'8--dc23

Manufactured in China

CPSIA Compliance Information: Batch BW18WM: For Further Information
contact Rosen Publishing, New York, New York at 1-800-237-9932

CONTENTS

Grace was on
a mission.

2

She had a very important job to do.

She couldn't do this job just anywhere. It had to be somewhere very special.

To get to this place, Grace had to swim for a long time. She would have to travel more than 1,000 miles (1,600 km)!

There were many dangers Grace had to avoid.
There were the sharks that followed her silently.

There were plastic bags that floated in the ocean, pretending to be jellyfish.

There were nets from fishing boats to dodge.

Grace even had to dive deep
to escape the propellers
of boats speeding past.

Grace stopped every now and then to eat the sea grass that grew in the shallow waters of the ocean. It was her favorite food.

Along the way, Grace saw some beaches littered with garbage that had washed up from the ocean.

Grace hoped that she would not find garbage where she was heading.

She had not been
to this special place
for more than
twenty years.

In fact, she had
not been there
since she was
a tiny baby.

Nobody told
her how to find
this place. Grace
just followed her instincts,
like her mother had before her.

She knew she must be getting close.
She could sense it.

There in front of her was the beautiful beach Grace had been looking for. It was where she had started her life.

It was perfect!

Other sea turtles thought it was perfect too. Grace gathered with them in the shallow waters off the beach to mate.

Then, ever so slowly, she dragged herself up the beach to above the shoreline.

Using her hind flippers, she dug a deep hole and laid nearly 200 eggs.

Then Grace covered her eggs,
returned to the ocean,
and swam away.

She would not see her babies
when they hatched months later.
They would have to make
their own way to the ocean.

But maybe, just maybe, in twenty years' time, Grace will be lucky enough to be on that very beach

when one of her daughters comes out of the water to lay her own eggs for the very first time.

GLOSSARY

dodge to move around something

hatch to come out of an egg

hind flippers the parts at the back of an animal that are used for swimming

instincts a way of acting without thinking about it

littered spread across an area in a messy way

mate when animals come together to produce young

mission an important job or assignment

propellers the part of a boat that spins and makes it move

sense to have a feeling; to notice

shallow not very deep

shoreline the line where a body of water and the shore meet

Dangers to Sea Turtles

Plastic bags

Sharks

Fishing nets

Boat propellers

Beach pollution